TABLE OF CONTENTS

CHAPTER 1
DON'T LOOK BACK!

Carlos headed down the long straightaway. It was the easiest part of the Del Rey Motocross Racecourse, but Carlos was still worried.

He knew what lay ahead. There was a series of three hairpin turns. Then there were two big jumps on the way to the finish line. That's not why he was worried. After all, Carlos had spent most of the last two years on this track.

No, Carlos was worried about something else.

The long straightaway was the last chance on the course to take a quick peek to see if anyone was coming up from behind. That's exactly what had Carlos worried.

He's got to be close, Carlos thought. Ricky is never too far behind.

Carlos couldn't see him, but he could sense that Ricky was there. He knew if Ricky was close, he'd soon be making a big move to win this race.

Don't look back, he thought. Looking back will slow you down!

Carlos knew it was risky, but he decided to look back anyway. He turned his head to look over his left shoulder.

Just then, Carlos felt the handlebars slip.

The front wheel had turned ever so slightly. Then the dirt track beneath Carlos's motocross bike had caught it.

So Carlos lost his balance a little. He jerked the bike back up.

He kept himself upright. But the bobble had cost him precious time.

He got back to full speed. Ricky was alongside him on the right. Carlos had made a big mistake by looking back. He had looked back over the wrong shoulder!

Now it was a race for the finish.

Carlos had the inside track on the first hairpin, which turned to the left. The short path allowed him to get past Ricky.

Carlos held his balance through the turn. He sprayed Ricky with dirt off his back tire.

Carlos knew the next
right. Being on the right
have the advantage.

Ricky caught him on tl
On the third and final tur
ahead. This time he sprayed Carlos with
dirt in the turn.

All that remained were two big jumps
and the finish line.

Carlos and Ricky were side by side, with
Ricky slightly ahead.

Carlos knew their bikes were about the
same speed.

The winner of this race would be the one
who handled the jumps the best.

Carlos held steady on his bike. He was
determined to beat Ricky this time.

sailed high off the first jump,
rider looked at the other. As their
es dropped back to earth, both landed
softly. Now the riders were running neck
and neck.

At the final jump, Carlos's bike hit a
small rut. He went airborne. His front tire
was turned slightly sideways. That had
happened to him many times before. Earlier
in a race it wouldn't make much difference.
But they were close to the finish line. Carlos
knew this mistake could cost him the race.

Ricky landed with his tire facing
straight ahead. He surged ahead toward
the checkered flag. Carlos was close, but
finished a tire's length behind him.

Looking back had cost Carlos the race.

CHAPTER 2
THE NATIONALS

As he rode past the finish line, Ricky raised a hand in victory. Carlos's head hung low as he pulled his bike over and shut down the engine.

In a matter of seconds, Ricky pulled up alongside Carlos. He popped his helmet off.

"A little nervous out there, Carlos?" Ricky said, grinning. "It's not like you to be looking over your shoulder like that."

"So what?" Carlos said, shaking his

head. "I was just checking to see where you were."

"I was beating you, that's where I was," Ricky shot back. "And that's three times in a row! Not that I'm keeping track."

"Very funny," Carlos said. "Just remember that I won the four times before that."

Ricky smiled. "That's why I like being your friend," he said. "Without you to compete against, how would I ever get better?"

"If I have to lose a race," Carlos replied, "it would be nice if someone other than my best friend beat me. That way, I could leave the track and not hear about it all night!"

Both boys laughed. "Seriously, though, you ran a nice race," Carlos said.

The boys bumped fists. "Thanks, man," Ricky said. "Let's go check the schedule and see when the next race is."

The boys walked back toward the track office.

Outside the office was a bulletin board. That's where Mr. Martin, the track owner, posted the schedule for the next month.

The boys practiced at the track all the time. They looked forward to the races that were held each weekend.

They were clearly the two best riders at the Del Rey track. Almost every race in their age group was won by one of them.

The boys reached the office. Mr. Martin was outside, taking down the last month's schedule.

"Looks like our timing is good," Carlos said. "Time for the new schedule to go up."

"Sorry, boys," Mr. Martin said. "I don't have the new schedule ready yet. I have to wait until I hear from the guy at Benson Motors."

"Benson Motors? That's the company that makes all the bike engines," Ricky said. "What do they have to do with the schedule?"

Mr. Martin looked down at the boys. He had a serious look on his face.

"You know, boys, I've owned this track a long time," he said. "I've tried to make it a first-class operation. One that good racers would really enjoy."

"Racers like us," said Ricky.

"Right," Mr. Martin said with a smile.

He went on, "Well, it appears somebody has finally noticed. Benson Motors wants to come here and watch some races. They are looking for riders they can sponsor for the Nationals."

If it was possible, Mr. Martin's smile grew even bigger. "I told them about the two of you," he said.

The boys' mouths dropped open.

They couldn't believe what they were hearing.

Both of them had become very strong racers. But neither of them had ever traveled to a regional event, let alone Nationals.

Getting to race in the United States Motocross Association Nationals would be a dream come true.

Being sponsored by a big company would be even better than that.

"Holy cow," Carlos said as the boys walked away. "Can you believe this? Nationals!"

"And being sponsored!" Ricky said. "Do you really think we're good enough to get a sponsorship?"

Just then, Mr. Martin called out to the boys. "Come back tomorrow morning," he shouted. "I should know everything by then."

CHAPTER 3
THE PACT

The boys weren't sure they could wait that long. Ricky's parents were out of town, so he was spending the weekend with Carlos's family. That meant a long night of talking and wondering about the potential to go to USMA Nationals.

The boys tried to take their minds off the Nationals by playing video games. But they started playing *Motocross Meltdown*, which got their minds on it even more.

Finally, they shut down the video game and went on the Internet. They wanted to get any information they could about the Nationals.

"Wow!" Ricky said. He looked closely at the website. "The Nationals are in Dallas. It would be pretty cool to go hang out there together."

"No kidding," Carlos replied. "I bet the track at Nationals is awesome. And if we had a sponsor, they would pay for the whole trip!"

That night, Carlos and Ricky barely slept.

They got up early the next morning. Carlos's mom gave them a ride down to the track in her pickup. They could practice and hear the news from Mr. Martin.

At the track, they hurried into Mr. Martin's office. He was sitting in his chair, talking on the phone. When he saw the boys, he motioned for them to come in.

"Oh, okay," Mr. Martin said into the phone. "You're sure that's the way you want to do it?" Mr. Martin seemed concerned, and a little confused.

"All right, all right," Mr. Martin said. "I'll get a sign-up sheet on the board. Thank you, Mr. Benson."

Mr. Martin hung up the phone. He didn't seem nearly as happy as he did the day before. "Well, boys," he said, "There's going to be a competition for the sponsorship."

"That's okay," Ricky said quickly. "We don't mind competing with other racers."

Carlos laughed in agreement.

"Well, you're not just going to be competing with other riders," Mr. Martin said. "You're going to be competing with each other."

"What?" yelled Ricky.

"Only one rider will get sponsored," said Mr. Martin.

Carlos and Ricky looked at each other.

Suddenly, both boys felt sick.

Finally, Carlos spoke. "What does that mean?"

Mr. Martin cleared his throat. "Benson Motors has a plan. They want me to hold a track championship," he said.

He paused. He looked from Carlos to Ricky, and then back.

"They want us to have a three-race series here at Del Rey," Mr. Martin went on. "There's also going to be a championship at the track over in Watkins. The rider who does the best in our races will have a race-off with the winner from the Watkins track. The winner of that gets the sponsorship."

Carlos swallowed hard. All of a sudden, he found it hard to even look at Ricky.

"When is all this going to happen?" Ricky asked.

"Well, it has to happen fast," Mr. Martin said. "We're going to hold all three races next weekend. Friday night, Saturday afternoon, and Sunday afternoon. Then the race-off against the Watkins track's winner will happen the following weekend."

Carlos and Ricky stood up to leave.

"Sounds good," Carlos muttered. But he wasn't sure he meant it.

"Yeah, sounds good," Ricky said.

"The sign-up sheet will go up later today," Mr. Martin said. "In the meantime, you guys better start practicing."

The boys walked out the door without speaking. Neither one of them was sure what to say.

They went to the locker room. There, they got dressed in their racing suits and grabbed their helmets. They walked slowly out toward their bikes.

Finally, Carlos couldn't stand the silence anymore. "Okay, so we can't both get sponsored," he said. "So let's make a pact."

"A pact?" Ricky said.

"Yeah, like a contract," Carlos replied. "Let's race each other the best we can, and whoever wins, wins. And whoever loses will help the other guy get ready for the race-off."

"All right," Ricky said. "I'm in." He cracked a little smile. The boys bumped fists, hopped on their bikes, and started the engines.

CHAPTER 4
BIKE TAGS

For the rest of the day, Ricky and Carlos raced hard.

They took very few breaks as they looked for ways to cut time in the hairpin turns.

They tried new ways to keep their balance through the jumps, and any other tricks that would result in a faster time.

As the day was coming to an end, neither boy wanted to be the first to leave the track.

They both knew that every minute on the track would help them get ready. And they didn't want the other guy to have an advantage.

It wasn't until Mr. Martin came out of the office and waved at them to come off the track that either rider shut down his engine.

Both boys were exhausted. They trudged away from the track and over to the office. The sign-up sheet was up now, and six other boys had already penciled their names in. One at a time, the boys put their names on the sheet.

They hardly talked as they put their helmets away and took off their racing suits. Carlos's mother was there to pick them up. The ride home was mostly silent.

At Carlos's house, Ricky gathered up his stuff.

His parents were back from their vacation. Ricky said goodbye and started toward the door.

"Hey, wait," Carlos called out. "Don't forget about our pact."

"Don't worry," Ricky said. "I won't forget." Then he turned and walked out the door.

Carlos couldn't help but wonder if their friendship could survive the races that lay ahead.

For the rest of the week, Carlos and Ricky barely spoke to each other.

They saw each other at the track all the time. But both of them were very businesslike.

They got to the track, dressed to race, and went out to work on their racing skills.

For the most part, they stayed away from each other on the track, too.

Neither one of them wanted the other to see what he was working on.

The less they knew about each other's racing plans, the better.

The track stopped being a fun place for the boys. They missed the time they hung out together.

Carlos started to wish none of this had happened.

Until now, the boys had competed against each other, but it had always been in fun.

Now, it seemed so serious.

It was the longest week of their lives.

When Friday finally came, both boys got to the track early and checked out their bikes.

Then they walked their bikes over toward the track office for inspection.

Mr. Martin was waiting there with another man. "Welcome to the first Del Rey Track Championships!" Mr. Martin exclaimed.

He smiled, and then said, "I hope you boys are ready for a great time and some great competition. This is Mr. Dylan from Benson Motors. They have asked him to be in charge of the championship races at our track."

Mr. Dylan stepped forward. He looked very professional.

"Boys, my job is to make sure the races are fair, so everyone has a chance to win," he said. "I'll be inspecting all of the bikes before the race starts. You can just leave your bike here, and come back for it in a half hour."

Carlos and Ricky walked away from the bikes. They both felt very tense and nervous.

Finally, Carlos decided to try to break up the tension. "You know they're going to catch that illegal engine you put on that bike of yours," he said.

Ricky shot a glare at Carlos. Then he realized his friend was only joking. "They'll probably find those illegal tires you use, too," Ricky said.

They both laughed.

"Hey, man," said Carlos, holding out his fist. "Good luck."

Ricky bumped Carlos's fist with his own. "Yeah, good luck."

The boys headed off in different directions.

Carlos walked into the locker room in the track office. He grabbed a soda. He waited there for a half hour, then headed back out to his bike.

Ricky was already there, bent over Carlos's bike. He was fiddling with something.

"Hey, Ricky," Carlos yelled out as he approached. Ricky stood up straight.

"Geez, don't scare me like that," Ricky said.

"Sorry," Carlos replied. "Whatcha doing?"

"I was just getting your tag off your bike for you," Ricky said. "They put tags on all the bikes to say they passed inspection."

Ricky handed Carlos his tag.

"Okay, cool," Carlos said.

Then Mr. Dylan walked over. "All right boys, let's get racing," he said.

Carlos, Ricky, and eight other boys walked their bikes toward the starting line.

Once they had lined up, they started their engines.

Carlos threw a leg over his bike and sat down. He felt ready to race. He gave his throttle a little squeeze, just to rev the engine. It sounded great.

Mr. Dylan walked over toward the starting line. Then he climbed up into the starter's tower.

He held out the green starting flag.

Carlos and Ricky revved their engines again. They nodded at each other to say good luck.

That's when Carlos noticed the smell.

Gasoline.

CHAPTER 5
RUNNING ON EMPTY

Carlos wasn't sure if the smell was coming from his bike.

There was always some kind of gasoline odor at the track. But this time it seemed very strong.

There was no time to check on it or to do anything about it.

Mr. Dylan lowered the green flag, and all of the racers took off.

Ricky bolted to the front, but Carlos was close behind.

The early part of the track had some easy curves and straightaways. Carlos did his best to keep up with Ricky.

But each time Carlos tried to accelerate, he smelled the strong scent of gasoline again.

Ricky moved a full bike length ahead and grabbed the inside line on the track.

That forced Carlos behind him. Carlos was taking a lot of dirt spray off the back of Ricky's bike.

Carlos and Ricky moved ahead of the rest of the racers quickly.

That made it a two-man race before the first lap was even complete.

With no other riders nearby, though, Carlos knew that the gasoline smell was coming from his bike. But what was causing it? A leak?

Carlos shot a quick glance down.

That's when he spotted the thin spray of gasoline coming from the gas line.

Carlos kept pushing to catch Ricky. He glanced down at his gas gauge. He was already down to half a tank.

There was very little chance that he'd be able to finish the race.

Still, Carlos rode on. He hoped to keep enough gas to finish the race.

Failing to finish would mean he'd be in tenth place heading into the second race. It would be almost impossible to win the sponsorship with such a bad start.

Carlos let Ricky pull away. Ricky was going to win this race easily.

Carlos just wanted to finish second.

He tried to hold on to second place. He watched his gas gauge as the gas supply disappeared.

All the while, he kept wondering how this could have happened. The bike had been in perfect shape.

The race was a little more than ten minutes long. Carlos's bike made it through the first ten minutes, but when the final two laps began, the bike began to sputter.

Just as Carlos reached the start of the final lap, his engine died.

All of the other racers cruised by him, fighting for second place.

Carlos suddenly remembered the scene before the race.

He remembered seeing his bike, and seeing someone bent over it. Ricky.

Could it be?

CHAPTER 6
ACCUSATIONS AND REVENGE

Carlos waited by the starter's tower for the race to end. Ricky cruised by first, well ahead of the rest of the field.

He seemed startled when he saw Carlos already standing there.

When Mr. Dylan climbed down from the tower, Carlos was ready with his questions. "Were the bikes protected during the inspection?" he asked. "Did anyone keep an eye on them?"

"Yes, we were watching them the whole time," Mr. Dylan said. "Why? What happened?"

"I've got a puncture hole in my gas line, and I ran out of gas," Carlos said.

"Well, those things happen," Mr. Dylan said. "Those tubes can pop sometimes."

Carlos looked down at the gas line. "Mr. Dylan, that hole is a little puncture, like a pin prick or a tiny nail or something," Carlos said. "It didn't just happen."

Mr. Dylan tried to calm Carlos down. "I'm sorry it happened to you in such an important race," he said.

"Yeah, well, I think I know how it happened," Carlos said.

He stormed off toward the track office.

Ricky was standing there, getting congratulated by the other riders for his first place finish.

Behind him, the standings were being posted. Ricky's name was at the top, with ten points. All the other riders were listed below him. The second-place rider had nine points, the third-place rider had eight, and so on.

At the bottom was Carlos's name, in tenth place, with one point. As Carlos approached, Ricky spotted him. "Hey, man, what happened?" Ricky said.

"Don't give me that!" Carlos shot back. "You know exactly what happened. Little hole in the gas line! Sound familiar?"

"What the heck are you talking about?" Ricky said.

"Come on," Carlos replied. Now he was walking straight at Ricky. "I saw you. I saw you messing with my bike. And then all of a sudden it has a gas leak."

Ricky was stunned. He couldn't believe what he was hearing.

"Carlos," Ricky said. Carlos was walking away. "Carlos! Come on, man! You know I would never do anything like that!" But Carlos was pretty sure he had. How else could he explain it?

Carlos knew his chances of getting the sponsorship were almost done. Even if he won the other two races, he'd still only have twenty-one points. If Ricky finished second both times and got nine points in each race, he'd finish with twenty-eight. There was almost no way for Carlos to catch up.

Still, Carlos repaired his gas line. He showed up the next day for the second race. He saw Ricky when they dropped the bikes off for inspection. Neither boy said a word.

When the other drivers walked away, Carlos stayed behind. He wasn't going to leave his bike this time.

Carlos stayed and watched the entire inspection by Mr. Dylan. When it was done, he walked his bike to the starting line. Soon, Ricky and the other drivers arrived. Carlos revved his engine. There was no smell of gasoline this time. He was ready.

When the flag dropped, Carlos was off to a fast start.

He grabbed the inside line and moved quickly out ahead of the other riders.

His bike was working perfectly, and he felt like he was in total control. Even if he couldn't win the sponsorship, Carlos wanted to win the final two races.

After a few laps, Carlos couldn't even hear the roar of any of the other riders' bikes. It was as if he was on the track by himself. When the first ten minutes were over, only two laps remained. Carlos felt in total control.

But as he cruised past the starting line, he saw something that startled him so much that he almost lost his balance.

It was Ricky, standing next to the starter's tower. His bike's back tire was flat. Ricky was shaking his fist and yelling as Carlos rode by.

CHAPTER 7
FRESH CLUES

Carlos kept his concentration. He won the race easily. When he rode under the checkered flag for the victory, Ricky was no longer there. Carlos put his bike away. Then he walked over to the track office to check the results of the race.

Before he could get there, however, Ricky confronted him.

"So, you thought you had to get even, huh?" Ricky challenged.

"Ricky, I didn't do anything to your bike," Carlos said. "Can't you see what's going on here?"

"Yes, I can," Ricky said. "You thought I sabotaged your bike, so you sabotaged mine. I know you stayed with the bikes during the inspection."

Ricky's bike had been sabotaged. So Carlos knew Ricky wasn't to blame for his gas leak.

He now believed that someone else was causing this.

"Ricky, calm down," Carlos said. "Think about it. Somebody doesn't want us to get to the race-off with the Watkins driver."

Ricky stopped and thought for a minute.

He wasn't sure what to believe.

"Look," Carlos said. "Let's say we both finish last. That means somebody else from Del Rey goes to the race-off. Most of the other guys here are just getting started with racing. That makes it pretty likely that the Watkins kid wins, right?"

Ricky's expression changed. He was starting to see Carlos's point.

"Ricky, I'm sorry I thought you sabotaged me," Carlos said. "I was wrong. But I didn't mess with your bike. Somebody's messing with both of us. We just need to find out who."

Ricky thought for a minute. Then he had an idea how to find out. "Let's check the race results at the other track. We might get a clue about who would want us to lose," he said.

RACE RESULTS

	Race 1 Points	Race 2 Points	Race 3 Points	Total Points
				12
Jamarr	6	6		12
Brian	4		8	11
Ricky	10		1	11
Carlos	1		10	11
Derek	9		2	1
James	8		3	
David	7		4	
Oliver	2		9	
Juan	5		5	
			7	
			3	

First, they needed to check the Del Rey standings. When they got to the track office, they couldn't believe what they saw.

Only two riders were ahead of them, and by only one point.

"Unbelievable!" Carlos shouted. "We still have a chance! If one of us finishes first, and the other finishes second, we'll be the top two riders!"

It was true. The rest of the riders all finished in a different order. So all of the riders were close together in the standings after two races. Carlos and Ricky had a chance.

"But it's not going to matter if we don't find out who's been messing with our bikes," Ricky said. "Let's go check out the Watkins race on the Internet."

Ricky and Carlos went into Mr. Martin's office and asked to use the computer. They told him their ideas. He seemed concerned.

"Well, something's definitely not right," Mr. Martin said.

Carlos found the Watkins track's website and looked up the race results. When the results popped up on the screen, they were amazed at what they saw.

The boy in first place had a familiar name: Jeremy Dylan.

"Does that say Dylan?" Ricky yelped. "As in, the same last name as the guy who is doing our inspections?"

"It sure does," Carlos said. "Looks like the Dylan family doesn't want us to race against their son."

CHAPTER 8
TEAMWORK

Mr. Martin wasn't so sure. "Boys, that can't be right," he said. "Mr. Dylan works for Benson Motors. He could probably get the company to sponsor his son just by asking. After all, his boss, Mr. Benson, is the man who is giving out the sponsorship."

"But who else could be doing this?" Carlos said. "He's the only one who could go near the bikes during the inspections."

"You've got a point," Mr. Martin said.

Carlos had an idea.

"Whoever is doing it, their plan isn't working, because we're still in the race," Carlos said. "That means they will probably try again. I know one thing for sure. I'm not taking my eyes off my bike until the race starts tomorrow."

Mr. Martin grinned. "I've got an idea," he said. Carlos and Ricky loaded their bikes into the back of Ricky's dad's truck. That would keep them safe for the night.

The next morning, they brought them back. They stayed with the bikes all morning.

Mr. Dylan called for inspections. The boys stayed with their bikes. "It's all right, boys," he said. "You don't need to stay here for the inspections."

"Okay, Mr. Dylan," Ricky replied. "We'll be back in half an hour."

The boys walked inside the track office. They climbed the stairs toward the storage area upstairs.

Up above the inspection area, Mr. Martin looked out the window of the storage room. He wasn't alone. Mr. Benson from Benson Motors was with him.

"I hope you're not wasting my time," Mr. Benson said.

"I hope we are," Mr. Martin said. "I would hate to think someone is sabotaging the riders at my track. But we have to make sure the contest is fair. Don't we?"

Mr. Benson nodded.

He watched from the window as Mr. Dylan inspected Ricky's bike.

He stared in amazement.

Mr. Dylan opened Ricky's gas tank and dropped in a tablet of some type. A moment later, he did the same thing to Carlos's bike.

Mr. Benson bolted down the stairs. The boys and Mr. Martin watched from above as he confronted Mr. Dylan.

None of them could hear what was being said, but Mr. Dylan's head lowered. After a few minutes, he walked away sadly.

When the boys came out, Mr. Benson was shaking his head.

"I just can't believe he went that far," Mr. Benson said. "He's been bugging me to sponsor his boy for a year. I told him I would, but only if his son was really the best rider in the area. That's why we had the contest."

Carlos and Ricky felt better that they had helped to solve the mystery, but they were unsure what would happen next.

"Mr. Martin told me all about you boys and he shared your racing times with me," Mr. Benson said. "I'd like to sponsor both of you at Nationals."

"Are you serious?" Carlos yelled. "That's awesome!"

The boys jumped up and down, giving each other high fives and yelling.

Suddenly, Ricky got serious.

He realized that what Mr. Dylan put into the gas tanks might wreck the engines of the bikes.

"Hey, we better empty out those gas tanks," Ricky said. "I don't know what he put in there, but it can't be good."

"That won't be necessary," Mr. Benson said. "Part of the sponsorship is a brand new Benson Motors cycle for each of you."

Once again, the boys cheered.

As they bounced away toward the parking lot, Carlos turned to Ricky.

"Hey, if we're both going to Nationals, we're going to need to make a new pact," Carlos said.

"Yeah? And what is it this time?" Ricky replied.

"If something happens to either of our bikes," said Carlos, "we won't blame each other."

"Something is going to happen to your bike, though," said Ricky.

"Huh?" Carlos was confused.

"It's going to come in right behind mine, man!" said Ricky. "Because I am going to win!"

"You think so?" said Carlos.

Nationals were coming, and Carlos and Ricky couldn't wait. They walked toward the lot, planning their victories.

ABOUT THE AUTHOR

Bob Temple lives in Rosemount, Minnesota, with his wife and three children. He has written more than thirty books for children. Over the years, he has coached more than twenty kids' soccer, basketball, and baseball teams. He also loves visiting classrooms to talk about his writing.

ABOUT THE ILLUSTRATOR

When Sean Tiffany was growing up, he lived on a small island off the coast of Maine. Every day, from sixth grade until he graduated from high school, he had to take a boat to get to school. When Sean isn't working on his art, he works on a multimedia project called "OilCan Drive," which combines music and art. He has a pet cactus named Jim.

GLOSSARY

accusation (ak-yooz-AY-shuhn) — a claim that someone has done something wrong

championship (CHAM-pee-uhn-ship) — a competition to determine the winner of an event

hairpin (HAIR-pin) — a sharply curved section of road, in a U shape

inspection (in-SPEK-shuhn) — a careful examination of something

motocross (MOH-tuh-kross) — a timed motorcycle race over a winding, hilly course

nationals (NASH-uh-nuhlz) — the event that determines a country's champion in a sport

revenge (ri-VENJ) — action that you take to pay someone back for harm done to you

sabotage (SAB-uh-tahzh) — to secretly hurt another person's chances of winning

sponsor (SPON-ser) — the person or group that pays for another to enter a contest

throttle (THROT-uhl) — the lever that controls the speed of a motocross bike

MORE ABOUT . . .

Motocross is one of a number of sports in which riders race on bikes over natural terrain, such as grass or dirt.

In fact, the word "motocross" comes from combining the words "motorcycle" and "cross-country."

Motocross races are generally short, between ten and twenty minutes.

The races can be run on entirely natural tracks or on ground that has been shaped into many jumps and turns.

~~~. . . . MOTOCROSS ~~~

Unlike many other types of bike racing, motocross racers start all together from a starting line.

There are many other types of competitions that are similar in some ways to motocross.

• **Bicycle motocross**, or **BMX**, is like motocross except that the riders are on specially designed bicycles, instead of motorcycles.

• **Supercross**, which is sometimes called **arenacross**, is like motocross except that it's held inside a sports arena. Usually, there are more jumps, and higher jumps, in supercross events than in motocross.

• **Freestyle motocross**, or **FMX**, is an event in which riders do tricks off jumps and are judged based on their tricks, not on their speed.

DISCUSSION QUESTIONS

1. Carlos assumed that Ricky had sabotaged his bike without being sure. What should Carlos have done before accusing his best friend?

2. Mr. Dylan was responsible for rigging the boys' bikes. What do you think Mr. Benson could have done to prevent it from happening in the first place?

3. Why do you think the sponsorship meant so much to the boys?

WRITING PROMPTS

1. Carlos and Ricky are best friends, but they also compete against each other. Have you ever competed against a friend? Write about what that was like.

2. Carlos accused Ricky of sabotaging his bike. Have you ever been wrongly accused of doing something? Write about it.

3. Mr. Dylan cheated in order to have his son win. Have you ever thought about cheating? What did you do? Write about it.

JAKE MADDOX

SLAM DUNK SHOES

STONE ARCH *Realistic Fiction*

Jamal's been asked to try out for a super-elite youth basketball team. His dad makes him a deal: If Jamal makes the team, he gets new shoes. But will the fancy new shoes really improve Jamal's game?

JAKE MADDOX

SNOWBOARD DUEL

STONE ARCH *Realistic Fiction*

Hannah and Brian have the run of Snowstream, a cool winter resort. But a new kid, Zach, starts a boys-only snowboard cross team. What will Brian do when he's forced to choose between Hannah and snowboarding?

INTERNET SITES

Do you want to know more about subjects related to this book? Or are you interested in learning about other topics? Then check out FactHound, a fun, easy way to find Internet sites.

Our investigative staff has already sniffed out great sites for you!

Here's how to use FactHound:

1. Visit *www.facthound.com*

2. Select your grade level.

3. To learn more about subjects related to this book, type in the book's ISBN number: **1598898450**.

4. Click the **Fetch It** button.

FactHound will fetch the best Internet sites for you!